DIARY

OF A
MINECRAFT
ZOMBIE

DIARY
OF A
MINECRAFT
ZOMBIE

*Zombie's Birthday
Apocalypse
Book 9*

SCHOLASTIC INC.

ISBN 978-1-338-06456-8

12 11 10 9 8 7 6 5 4   17 18 19 20 21

Printed in the U.S.A.   40

First Scholastic printing, September 2016

Monday

Just a few more weeks until Halloween, and I can't wait!

Not just because it's my favorite holiday.

It's also my birthday!

I'm gonna be 13 years old.

Now, I know that's not a big deal, especially since Zombies can live forever.

But it's a big deal to me.

You see, being 13 means that I'll be a teenager now.

And being a teen means I can get a little more respect around here.

…And I need it too.

Because you know, being a 12 year old noob in middle school can be pretty painful.

Especially because those wedgies are starting to leave some serious marks.

…Not to mention what getting thrown into the dumpster is doing to the shape of my head.

I only wish I could get more respect at home.

But I think my Mom and Dad are always going to treat me like a baby Zombie.

Like this morning, my Mom made my lunch for school...

Now, I know that doesn't sound that bad.

But she always makes these mob baby cookies to let me know she loves me.

Talk about embarrassing.

When I open my lunchbox at school the other mob kids are always teasing me about it.

"What's the matter *wittle* baby Zombie? Do you need a *wittle* milk to go with your cookies?"

Then the whole cafeteria starts laughing at me.

It seems like I have a sign that says "LOSER" painted on my forehead every time I open my lunchbox.

Not to mention the one on my back that says, "I WANT A BIG, FAT WEDGIE RIGHT NOW."

Now I would throw the cookies away before I get to school.

But they taste really good.

...Especially with milk.

But being 13 has its perks.

Like, I'm supposed to get a raise in my allowance.

But knowing my Mom and Dad, it's not going to be much.

Their rule is that I'm supposed to get a dollar for every year that I'm older.

So for my 13th birthday, I get...you guessed it...13 dollars.

There's not much a Zombie can do with 13 dollars every month.

So I just spend it on what's really important, like cake!

Now I know I should be saving up my allowance like a responsible young Zombie.

But with only 13 dollars, I can't even afford to pay attention.

But it's ok. The really cool thing about being 13 is that my Dad said that I could get a job.

So I don't have to survive on a measly 13 dollars every month.

I'm going to get a job and get paid the real 'Benjamins.'

I just have to figure out what I'm going to do for work.

Right now the only thing I'm really good at is collecting boogers.

But I hope I get some money for my birthday too.

If I do, I want to buy a new video game for my ScareStation 465.

My parents gave me a ScareStation 465 for winning the Spelling Bee last month.

And it's awesome!

And there's a new video game Steve told me about that I really want to get.

He said it's called HALO 3000—Zombie Apocalypse Edition.

Sounds so cool! I can't wait.

Speaking of my birthday, I need to come up with a really cool theme for my birthday party.

Since its Halloween, I usually have a Halloween party for my birthday.

But the Halloween parties my Mom and Dad put together are kind of lame.

They're not scary at all.

Last year, we had a "My Little Zombie Pony" Halloween Party.

Everybody had to dress up like a Zombie Pony.

Lame.

This year I want to do something really scary. Something to tell the world that I'm a big Zombie now.

Like...a pool party!

Zombies really hate water, so that should give them a good scare.

But maybe I shouldn't. I just remembered that my buddy Slimey is terrified of water. Especially after what happened to his uncle.

Or maybe I could do a skateboard party!

Naw… Knowing Skelee he'll probably fall down and break a bone or something.

Maybe I could do a surprise party?

I could just act surprised when everybody jumps out.

Well, maybe not. I think that would be really bad for Creepy…and that would be really bad for the rest of us.

I got it!

We can do a Harry Potter party!

That movie really gave me the creeps.

Everybody can dress up like those really scary kids from Hogwarts.

We can ride around brooms, wave magic wands, and talk in English accents and stuff.

And I can dress up like Harry Potter. I just have to get a uniform, some glasses, and carve a lightning bolt on my head.

Wow, this is going to be the best birthday party ever!

Tuesday

Today, I went to see Steve to tell him about my birthday party idea.

I found him in the forest, and he looked like he was looking for something.

Perfect time to try out my new scaring skills, I thought.

So I snuck up behind him and...

"HYEEEEEAAAAAAHHHHHUURRRGHHHH HZZZOOWWIIIIEEEEE!!!!!"

"Oh, hey Zombie."

Man, I'm getting rusty.

"Hey, Steve. Whatcha doing?"

"I'm just looking for a villager. Some of the folks in my village said that he went out to the forest to look for pumpkins and he never came back."

"That's weird."

"Yeah, he's been gone for a few days now."

"No, I meant that it's weird he went to look for pumpkins. I usually stay away from those things. Aren't they dangerous?"

"What do you mean?"

"Well, when I was a baby Zombie, I used to really love pumpkin pie. But then my Dad said that if I eat too much pumpkin, then I'll turn into one. Kind of like doughnuts."

Steve just looked at me...confused.

"That is weird," he said.

"But, hey Steve, I wanted to tell you about my birthday party idea."

"Are you doing the 'My Little Zombie Pony' party again this year? Cause I got a really nice Rainbow Dash stick-on tattoo I want to wear," Steve said snickering.

"Ha ha, not funny. Naw, this year I wanted to make it really, really scary. It's going to be the scariest Halloween party ever. This year I'm doing a Harry Potter Party!"

Steve just looked at me...confused.

"Yeah, we're going to carry books, wear uniforms, wave wands and everything."

Steve still looked confused.

"And I'm going to be Harry Potter. By the way, how good are you at carving Zombie skulls?"

All of a sudden we heard a noise.

"Hey, I think that's him," Steve said.

When we looked through the trees, we saw a villager, but instead of a big head and long nose, this villager had a pumpkin on his head.

"Why is he running around crazy and waving his hands in the air like that?" I asked Steve.

"I don't know, but I've got to bring him back to the village."

"See, my Dad was right. I told you that if you eat too much pumpkin, you'll turn into one."

Steve had that confused look on his face again and said, "I'll see you later, Zombie."

Then the villager with the pumpkin head ran off, and Steve chased after him.

Villagers are so weird, I thought.

I've always wondered why Steve isn't weird like them. Come to think of it, it's kind of weird that Steve doesn't have a long nose either.

Does Steve even have a nose?

Whoa.

Oh well, time to get some stuff together for my birthday party.

Oh man, I can't wait!

Wednesday

Today at Scare School, we went on a field trip to the Mob Science Museum.

Every month they have a different theme. Usually it's kinda lame, but sometimes they do some really cool stuff.

One time they talked about the science of 'spontaneous combustion.' Creepy really liked that one. Especially when they talked about how you can use Creeper poop to make cool fireworks.

Another time they talked about Skeletons. I thought Skelee would really like it. But he told me that the exhibit was lame compared to the crazy stuff he sees when he visits his relatives.

But this month's theme was about Halloween.

They had an exhibit about the history of Halloween that I really liked.

It said that Halloween is the biggest national holiday for Minecraft Mobs everywhere. They even take a day off of work and close the schools to honor this special day.

But it said that human villagers don't appreciate Halloween that much. They still have to work and go to school on Halloween.

Man, it must really stink to be a villager.

But my favorite part of the exhibit talked about the Science of Pumpkins.

It said that pumpkins were blocks that grow in most Overworld biomes.

I tried to find out if what my Dad said about turning into a pumpkin was true. But when I asked the Zombie lady giving the tour, she just gave me a strange look.

There was one thing she said at the end of the exhibit that seemed kinda weird though. She said…

About 500 years ago, a rare fungus infected all of the pumpkins in a small mob village. It caused all those mobs exposed to the fungus to lose all control and behave in an erratic and strange manner.

Those infected attacked and bit others, and the infection spread from village to village. It did not matter whether you were mob or human, all could be infected with the disease.

Those infected would be identified by their strange behavior and the distinct large pumpkin that spawned to cover their heads.

It has been theorized in scientific circles that this pumpkin fungus outbreak was the ultimate cause of the last Zombie Apocalypse…

Whoa!

She even showed us an old picture of one of the infected…

Man, I'm glad I wasn't around 500 years ago. That would've been so scaaaarryyy!

Anyway, all I care about right now is my birthday party, and how cool it is going to be.

Which reminds me, I need to start inviting the kids at school to my party.

I wonder if I should just invite the cool kids...

I mean, now that I'm going to be 13, I'm going to need a new set of friends to go with my new image, right?

Thursday

I started inviting some of the cool kids at school to come to my birthday party today.

But it was kind of weird that every time I asked any of them, they just started laughing.

I guess that means that they really want to be there.

I started thinking about Creepy, Skelee and Slimey.

Maybe I shouldn't invite the guys this year, I thought.

You see, the guys are still only 12 years old.

And in school, a lot of the cool kids think they're noobs.

But it would be kind of weird not having them at my birthday party.

I mean, they've been coming to my birthday party ever since I was a baby Zombie.

I remember first meeting Skelee at my 6th birthday party.

I was swinging a stick at my Ender Dragon piñata when I accidentally knocked Skelee's head off.

I thought I was in big trouble until I saw that Skelee was laughing.

"What are you laughing at?" I asked him.

"I don't know. I guess this is what it means to 'laugh your head off,'" he said.

We've been best friends ever since.

I met Slimey at his cousin Cube's birthday party.

He was really small back then.

I remember I couldn't find a place to sit so I just sat on a little green table next to the bathroom.

I accidentally sat on Slimey by mistake.

We've been best buds ever since.

Meeting Creepy for the first time was really funny too.

Creepy was always quiet, and he got really nervous around other kids.

One day, in first grade, Skelee, Slimey and I went up to him and started talking.

He started hissing and flashing and stuff.

We didn't know what he was doing, but we thought it was so cool.

I think he was surprised we didn't run away, so he calmed down.

We poked him a few times to get him to start hissing and flashing again.

Yeah, we weren't really smart back then.

But we've been best friends ever since.

Man, what am I thinking?

I need my best buds at my party no matter how old they are. And I don't care how "uncool" the kids at school think they are.

All I know is that I can always count on my best friends to come and support me on my birthday.

Plus, if nobody else shows up, it won't be so embarrassing.

Friday

The weirdest thing happened today.

After dinner, my Dad got a call from the Nuclear Waste Plant he works at. He said there was an emergency at the factory.

"Hey Dad, is everything all right?"

"No worries, son. I just need to head over to the plant. It seems like they had another accident in the Deadly Fungus Containment lab."

Man, even though my Dad works in a Nuclear Waste Plant, he really makes his job sound so cool.

"When will you be back, honey?" Mom asked.

"Oh, it will just take a few hours, but don't stay up."

After Dad left, I started talking to Mom about all my plans for my birthday party.

"…And we're going to have brooms, and wands, and books and uniforms and everything…"

"It sounds kind of expensive, Zombie. Are you sure you don't want to come as a Zombie Pony like you did last year? I think your costume still fits."

"No way, Mom. Plus, I'm looking for a job so that I can pay for it. You won't have to pay for a thing."

"Oh, OK. By the way, don't forget that your father and I are going to be a little late for your party this year. We need to take your little brother Wesley and his friends out trick-or-treating. It's our turn this year to take Wesley's pre-school class trick-or-treating around the neighborhood."

Awesome! I was counting on it.

You see, you can't be cool and have your parents at your birthday party. So this was my chance to keep them from ruining it. I'll just make sure the cool kids come early and leave before my parents get back.

"Don't worry, Mom. Take as long as you want. Me and the guys will just play some video games until you and Dad get back."

"Yeah, I guess you are a big Zombie now," she said as she gave me her usual embarrassing Mom smile.

I kinda felt a little weird about not telling my Mom the truth, though.

But technically I didn't lie; I just left out the part that I invited the whole school to come to my party.

…But then why do I still feel so weird about it?

Saturday

I went to go see my ghoulfriend Sally today.

I was kind of bummed that she couldn't make it to my birthday party.

But she said that every year for Halloween she and her parents take a trip to the Transylvanian Biome. She said they're supposed to have the coolest Halloween Parties over there.

The Transylvanian Biome is also where the Zombie Royal Family comes from. They're supposed to be really special Zombies.

I think Sally said they were called Vampires.

"Hey Zombie!"

"Hey Sally. Getting ready for your trip?"

"Yeah, I can't wait. It's going to be so much fun running into some of the Vampires. I might even see some Werewolves and even Mummies."

"I know what Mummies are. But what are Werewolves?"

"Oh, my Dad said that Werewolves used to be like a Vampire's pet. But they're highly civilized now."

"Whoa."

"Yeah, but they have a lot of drama."

"Really?"

"Yeah, one time I heard a story of a Werewolf named Jacob that fell in love with the girlfriend of a Vampire named Edward. And she was human, but she wanted to be a

Vampire. But the Werewolf didn't want her to be a Vampire because he wanted her to be a Werewolf, and then..."

"Wow. I think I just got dizzy."

Man, and I thought I had a lot of drama in my life...

"So what did you decide to do for your birthday?" Sally asked. "Are you going to do the 'My Zombie Pony' party again this year? If you are, I can lend you my real Zombie pony and you can ride it to your party. You can make a really big entrance."

"No way. No more Zombie ponies for me. This year I'm going to have the scariest birthday party ever. I'm doing a Harry Potter party."

"Whoa. I had a friend that had a Harry Potter birthday party one year. It was really scary. One Zombie boy even came as the funny looking Weasley boy. It gave me nightmares for weeks. Great choice."

"Yeah, I'm coming as Harry Potter. But I still need to figure out how to carve a lightning bolt on my..."

"*SALLY DEAR, THE ZOMBIE TAXI IS HERE. WE NEED TO START HEADING OUT TO THE SCAREPORT.*"

"Oh, that's my Mom. Sorry Zombie, I have to go. But have a great birthday party. I'm going to miss you."

Then she and her family jumped into a car to head out to the Scareport.

I was just standing there with the butler.

"Would you care for some lemonade, Mr. Zeke?"

"It's Zack."

Sunday

I went to see Steve today to see if he could help me prepare for my birthday party.

This time I found Steve making some weapons on his crafting table.

"Hey Steve."

"Hey Zombie, what's sizzling?"

"Nothing. The sun's not up yet."

"No, I mean what's cooking?"

"Well, my Mom's making some rotten Mushroom stew for dinner if you want some."

"No, I mean what's happening?"

"Oh, nothing much. Just getting ready for the best party ever. WHOOOOAAA!!!"

"Oh yeah, how's that coming?"

"Really good. I invited all the cool kids at school and they're all coming! I didn't think they would, but whenever I invited them they laughed so hard, it looked like they were really looking forward to it."

Steve just looked at me with that confused look he makes a lot.

"What's up with you? What's with all the weapons?" I asked Steve.

"Well, it seems that a lot more villagers are missing. I need to go into the forest and find out what's going on."

"No problem. Hey, whatever happened to that crazy villager with the pumpkin head we saw a few days ago? Did you catch him?"

"Naw. He was running too fast. Actually, I've never seen a villager run that fast before."

"Yeah, I always thought that villagers didn't have any legs," I said. "Whenever I look at them, all I ever see is a head, a big nose, some arms and a robe."

"Yeah, well something is going on, and I need to find out what it is," Steve said, determined.

I was going to ask Steve to help me make decorations for my birthday party. But he was really serious about finding those missing villagers.

But that's OK. I guess that's what Moms are for.

Monday

Today I was trying to think of some cool Halloween games we can play at my birthday party.

Last year the Halloween games we played were sort of...well, lame.

We did the usual stuff like:

Bobbing for Shrunken Heads

Torch Tag

Pin the Bone on the Skeleton—We ran out of bones, but I'm glad Skelee was there. He really saved the day.

Spider Web Climbing

Witch Toss—My neighbor, the witch, really didn't appreciate that game very much.

35

Enderman Bingo

Grab the Ghost

And Slime Bowling—Really hard game, but it was kind of fun.

But this year, I want to do some really scary games that will give some mob kids nightmares.

Steve told me about some games that he played when he was a kid. When he told me about them I got so scared I couldn't sleep for days.

But they sounded like the kind of terrifying games I want to have at my party.

Games like:

Duck, Duck, Goose—This one creeped me out...

Pin the Tail on the Donkey—I'm still trying to figure out why they would take the tail off of a donkey just to put it back on. So strange... but cool!

Twister—Just thinking of human kids twisted up in strange positions makes me want to hurl. Awesome!

3-Legged Race—This one doesn't seem so scary, especially since there's a 3-legged kid in my school that would probably win every time.

Origami—I was too scared to even ask Steve what this was...

So with these games, I'm all set for my party.

My favorite one is the 'Origami' game. I don't know what it is, but it sounds exotic...and deadly.

Man, these games are going to give the kids that come to my party a scare they'll never forget.

Sweet!

I was thinking about bringing Steve's Plants Vs Zombies game to my party too.

But maybe I shouldn't.

Last time we showed it, one of the kids at the party lost his head.

Poor guy. Haven't heard from him in a long time.

He was a real talker too.

He doesn't say much nowadays.

Naah, I think I'll just keep it real simple.

But it's still going to be the best birthday party ever!

Tuesday

When I was walking home from school today I noticed that people in the neighborhood were putting up Halloween decorations around their houses.

One of my neighbors put up a scene of some human kids playing in the park.

It was terrifying.

Another one of my neighbors put up a scene of a group of humans having a barbecue.

It was so scary that I felt the maggots on the back of my neck stand up.

But the most disturbing one was on the lawn of Ms. Ursula, the witch.

She actually had a life-sized human clown on her yard!

It looked like it wanted to just jump out and eat your brains or something.

So wrong...

But man, I wonder if I can borrow that clown for my birthday party. That thing will scare the maggots right out of the kids!

I wanted to walk up to Ms. Ursula's house to ask her to borrow it. But I was too scared to walk in front of that clown monster. I just kept imaging it jumping out and eating my brain.

Man, I don't think I'll be able to get that clown's face out of my head.

Just… So wrong…

Wednesday

They had a special mob school assembly today and gathered all the mobs from all over the school together in the auditorium.

Then they showed us a film about what to do in case of a Zombie Apocalypse.

I didn't understand why they were showing it. It's not like we're going to have a Zombie Apocalypse any time soon.

Plus, I didn't understand what all the fuss was about. I kind of think that if Zombies were to take over the world, it would really improve our social status.

"Now you may be asking yourself what all the Zombie Apocalypse fuss is about..." the movie said.

Wow, I was just thinking that...

"You might even be thinking that a Zombie Apocalypse would probably improve your social status..."

Hey, how'd they do that?

"But in a true Zombie Apocalypse, Zombies go stark, raving mad and revert back to their primitive instincts. That means the end of Zombie civilization as we know it...which means no more video games and no more cake!"

Whoa! That's crazy.

"Just...BRAINS!"

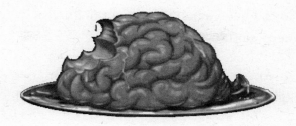

A bunch of the kids in the auditorium gasped. Another bunch of kids hurled. All the Endermen kids teleported. Some of Creeper kids started hissing and flashing. Even the Ghast kids started floating and wailing.

The whole auditorium went crazy!

The principal had to stop the assembly and send all of the kids back to their classrooms.

"Hey Skelee, what was all that about?"

"Well, they said it was supposed to be some kind of school Mob History Appreciation event," he said.

"Guys, I have a bad feeling about this," Creepy said.

"Do you think that we're going to have another Zombie Apocalypse?" Slimey asked.

Then we all looked at each other...

"PPFFFFFTTT!!! No way. There hasn't been a Zombie Apocalypse in like 500 years," I said.

Then we all started laughing and went back to class.

Thursday

After school today, I went to go see Steve, to see how he was doing.

I went to our usual hangout spot, but for some reason he wasn't there.

Then I looked in all of the places that he usually hangs out, but I couldn't find him there either.

I ran into Alex, who was out punching trees.

"Hey Alex. Have you seen Steve anywhere?"

"Oh, hey Zombie. No, I haven't seen him in a few days."

PUNCH. PUNCH. PUNCH.

"Do you know where he went?" I asked her.

"Well, he said that he was going to go find some missing villagers, but I haven't seen him since."

PUNCH. PUNCH. PUNCH.

Maybe he's still out searching, I thought.

"Oh OK. If you see him tell him I said hi," I said.

"Will do, Zombie dude," Alex said as she went back to punching her tree.

PUNCH. PUNCH. PUNCH. POP!

"Yeah!" Alex said.

I still don't understand why humans make such a fuss about punching trees.

So weird.

Friday

The coolest thing happened today!

When I was walking home from school, I noticed that Old Man Jenkins was dusting his old Zombie horse.

As I walked by I saw Mr. Jenkins bend over to pick up his brush.

All of a sudden I heard, "CRRAACCK!"

"OUCH!"

"Mr. Jenkins, are you alright?"

"Oh, it's just my old bones acting up again. But I could use a hand."

So I tried to help him straighten up when suddenly I heard, "CRRAACCKK, POP! THUMP!"

Uh oh.

Old Man Jenkins just broke into two pieces and his top half fell to the floor.

"Don't just stand there, get me up," Mr. Jenkins said.

So I helped get Mr. Jenkin's top half on his legs that were still standing.

"This is a young Zombie's game," he said looking at me. "Hey Zombie, how would you like a job?"

"A job? That's awesome!"

I was so happy I jumped up for joy, and Mr. Jenkins' top half fell to the floor again.

"THUMP!"

"Oh, sorry Mr. Jenkins," I said.

I helped Mr. Jenkins get his top half back on his legs that were still standing, again.

"Don't worry about it, Zombie. But I could sure use your help in taking care of my Zombie horse, Ed."

"Whoa, that would be great," I yelled as I threw my hands up in excitement.

"THUMP!"

Down went Old Man Jenkins again.

"Oh, I'm really sorry, Mr. Jenkins."

"Err... That's OK, Zombie."

I went to go pick him up again.

"No, no...err...That's OK, Zombie, I'll stay right here," Mr. Jenkins said as he leaned against his still standing legs.

"So whatdya say? Can you help an old Zombie take care of his Zombie horse?"

"Yes I can!" I said.

Wow, I'm going to have a job, which means that I'm finally going to make some real money.

Mr. Jenkins said I could start right away too. That means that I can make enough money to buy my Harry Potter costume for my birthday party.

Sweet!

Maybe I can even buy that life-sized clown from Ms. Ursula the witch, I thought.

Oh man, life couldn't get any better.

Saturday

"I'm sorry, son, but the answer is no."

"Waaaaahhhhh!!!"

"Zombie, taking care of a Zombie horse is a big responsibility. We just feel like you're too young for that right now."

"But you promised that I could get a job! Waaaaahhhhh!!!"

"Yes, but we meant something small, like cleaning the yard or delivering some mob newspapers."

"That's not fair!" I said as I ran to my room.

I don't know what my parents are talking about. I can take care of a Zombie horse. It's not like I haven't taken care of a pet before.

I mean, if my pet squid was still alive, I know I could've taken good care of it. How hard can a Zombie horse be?

Man, what am I going to do? I need a job quick so I can make enough money to buy my Harry Potter costume.

Hmmm. Maybe I can prove to my parents that I can take care of a Zombie horse after all.

I'll just make believe that I'm going to visit some friends, and go see Mr. Jenkins instead. And after taking care of Ed the Zombie horse for a few days, my parents will see that I can do it. They're going to have to say it's OK.

But man, I really hate lying to my parents.

Well, I guess it's not lying if I just tell them that I'm going to hang out with my friend Ed. Zombie horses can be friends too, I guess.

I still feel a little weird about it though.

I think I'm gonna take a nap.

Sunday

"**A**uthorities are puzzled over the sudden disappearance of some of the residents of Mob Village. Some believe that the residents are just visiting their relatives in other biomes. Others think they are just hibernating for the winter. While some even believe that they have been abducted by aliens to be probed and experimented on..."

That's all I heard as I came down from my room this morning.

"What are they talking about, Mom?"

"Well, it seems that some of the residents of Mob Village have disappeared."

"That's strange. Is it anybody we know?" my Dad asked.

"Well, Ms. Ursula the witch hasn't been seen since she put that hideous clown in front of her yard," my Mom said.

"Well, maybe the clown got her," Dad said laughing.

All of a sudden my little brother Wesley burst out crying.

"WAAAAAAAAHHHH!!!"

"Ooooh dear," was all Dad could say as he tried to calm Wesley down.

"Honey, you shouldn't have said that. You know how scared Wesley is of C—L—O—W—N—S," Mom said.

"Da clown is gung to get me!" Wesley cried.

"WAAAAAAAAAHHHH!!!"

I took my bowl of Booger Flakes and went to my room.

It's weird that people are missing from our village. What's even weirder is that's what was happening in Steve's village.

And where is Steve anyway? I haven't seen him for almost a week.

Hmmm. So weird.

But then I realized that with Ms. Ursula gone, I could borrow her clown for my party.

Sweet!

But how am I going to get that monster out of her yard and bring it over here? Especially without getting my face bitten off by that thing?

I would ask Steve, but he's not around.

I guess I can ask the guys to help me out.

Monday

After school today, my Mom took me and my little brother to get our Halloween Costumes.

We decided to go to "Zombies R Us" because they have some of the scariest costumes ever.

We searched for a long time, and I finally found the Harry Potter costume I was looking for.

But it cost 80 bucks!

"Please Mom! I can do more chores around the house, I promise!"

"I'm sorry, Zombie, but that is just too much money to spend on a costume that you're only going to wear for one day out of the year."

"But I'll wear it every day. I promise. I'll even to go to school with it."

"Zombie, that doesn't make sense. You'll look ridiculous going to school in that. I'm sorry but the answer is no."

All my hopes and dreams just went out the window.

Man, what am I going to do?

I guess I'm going to have to figure out a way to make my own Harry Potter costume. It's probably gonna be real hard too. I still haven't even figured out how to carve a lightning bolt on my head.

So we just spent the rest of the time shopping for a costume for my little brother Wesley.

As we were looking around, I saw a crowd of people standing around a display that had a large object covered in a black curtain.

It was inside a glass box that was locked with like 20 padlocks.

Then, around the glass box there were two big fat chains that were locked together with a big lock.

And in front of the glass box there were two security guards that were dressed in riot gear.

Man, I just had to find out what was in there.

I decided to ask the security guard what was inside the box.

"Inside this box is the scariest costume ever created in all of Minecraft," the security guard said.

"Hey can I see it?"

"I'm sorry but you must be accompanied by an adult in order to get a peek at this

64

monstrosity. It is just too dangerous for a young Zombie's eyes to see alone."

I ran over to my Mom to get her to ask the guard to let us see what was inside the box.

"I don't know, Zombie, it looks dangerous."

"But I'm almost 13, Mom. I can take it."

I guess she felt guilty for not getting me the Harry Potter costume, so she said yes.

I really wanted to get a picture of it too, so I borrowed my Mom's camera.

So, my mom and the rest of the crowd convinced the guards to let us see it.

The guards started to take off the two big chains that were around the glass box. Then, as they were opening the 20 padlocks, a bigger crowd started to gather around the display.

Then they opened the big glass box and took out the large object covered in the black curtain.

"Before we remove this curtain, we need to warn parents to cover the eyes of their young children. Also, if you are elderly, we are required to inform you that the sight of this costume has been known to cause convulsions, memory loss and temporary blindness," the security guard said.

The guard put his hand on top of the container and took a big gulp. The other guard stood back in a crouching position, holding up his riot shield.

It felt like it took forever for him to finally take off the curtain. But, I had my camera ready to capture the moment.

With a quick movement, the security guard removed the curtain off the container.

Everyone gasped. Some people screamed. A Skeleton Mom fainted right on the spot.

I stood there looking, but for some reason I couldn't feel my legs.

I wanted to move, but I was frozen in place.

All I could do was press the button on the camera, and there was a big flash.

Then everything went black.

Tuesday

My Mom made me stay home from school today to recover from yesterday's traumatic events.

I woke up kind of groggy. The weirdest thing was that I couldn't remember hardly anything that happened yesterday.

"What happened, Mom?"

"Good morning, Zombie. How are you feeling?"

"I feel a little dizzy, but I guess I'm OK."

"Do you remember anything that happened yesterday?"

I tried but everything was really fuzzy.

"Not really. I just remember we were looking for Wesley's costume and then next thing I know, I woke up this morning."

"Well, it was quite an evening. But the good thing is that we finally found a costume for Wesley."

"Really? What'd he get?"

"At first they didn't want to sell it to me until I signed a waiver of liability. But Wesley really wanted it, so I went ahead and bought it for him. They gave me a really good price for it too."

"What does it look like?"

"Well, you took a picture with my camera. It should still be in there."

I grabbed my Mom's camera from her rotten flesh purse. I scrolled through the pictures for about a minute until I saw the most terrifying thing I had ever seen.

And then everything went black...

Wednesday

I woke up this morning and got ready for school.

For some reason I was still having a hard time remembering what happened the day before.

It's a good thing I write everything in my journal, or I would forget everything.

I guess that's the drawback of having a Zombie brain the size of a pea.

So, I decided to walk to school today instead of taking the bus. I just needed to clear my head.

All of a sudden, when I was about to cross the street, some really big Zombie Army trucks whizzed right by me down the street.

That's weird, I thought. *I guess they must be having some kind of Zombie parade or something.*

When I got to school I saw a poster that said that we were going to have a Scariest Costume Contest next week at our school.

But what really caught my eye was that the winner of the Scariest Costume Contest would get a $50 gift certificate for… Zombies R Us!

Oh man, with a $50 gift certificate and the money I make from taking care of Old Man Jenkin's horse, I should have enough to buy my Harry Potter Costume for my birthday party!

Man, my luck is turning around.

Now I just have to figure out how I'm going to win the Scariest Costume Contest.

But what could I wear?

C'mon think, Zombie, think…

Thursday

Today I ran into Big Mouth Jeff in the school cafeteria.

He was bragging to a bunch of mob kids that he was going to win the Scariest Costume Contest at school.

"I'm gonna wear a costume that's so scary that they're going to have to close the school down for weeks," he said, "Too many kids are gonna be in therapy."

I couldn't let him get away with that so I had to say something!

"Oh yeah, well my costume is so scary that it'll make a Creeper poop fireworks."

"Oooooh!" the kids in the cafeteria said.

But Jeff had a comeback...

"Oh yeah, well my costume is so scary it'll make a Skeleton grow its skin back."

"Oooooh!" the kids said.

And I had a comeback of my own...

"Oh yeah, well my costume is so scary it'll make a Wither grow an extra head."

"Oooooh!" everybody said.

Then Jeff said...

"Oh yeah, well my costume is so scary it'll make a Slime walk on water."

"Oooooh!" everybody said.

Then I said...

"Oh yeah, well my costume is so scary I have to go trick-or-treating over the phone...and it's still scary!"

"Whoooaaahh!" the kids said.

Then Jeff said...

"Oh yeah, well, my costume is so scary, it makes onions cry."

And I said...

"Well, my costume is so scary, my Mom has to feed me with a slingshot."

Then Jeff said...

"Oh yeah, well my costume is so scary that when I threw a boomerang it didn't want to come back."

We went on like this for about 15 minutes. Then the bell rang for our next class.

Man, now I really need to get a scary costume. Otherwise I'm going to lose my $50 Zombies R Us gift certificate to Big Mouth Jeff.

…And then I won't be able to get my Harry Potter costume.

Man, what am I going to do?

C'mon think, Zombie, think!

Man, I bet if Steve was around he'd know what to do…

Friday

After school I went to go see if maybe Steve had come back from searching for the missing villagers.

But when I went to our usual hangout spot, he still wasn't there.

I decided to go to Steve's village to see if I could find him there.

I usually don't like going to Steve's village.

Especially since the last time I went, they chased me away with pitchforks and torches.

But I needed to find out what happened to Steve, so I went anyway.

When I got to Steve's village, there was nobody there.

It was like a ghost town, but without the ghosts.

I even went up to a villager's door and knocked, but nobody answered.

Usually you hear someone screaming and yelling and stuff.

But this time I didn't hear anything.

Then, I went to see if there were any farmers around.

But when I got to the farm, there was nobody there either.

I thought I saw somebody far away. But when I got close, it was just a stick man with a pumpkin head and a shirt full of straw, covered in birds.

I tried to talk to him, but he wasn't very social.

When I was leaving, suddenly I saw a villager run into the forest.

I followed him into the forest and peeked at him from behind the bushes.

What was weird is that he had a pumpkin on his head too. Except he had arms and legs, but no straw in his shirt.

He was running around all crazy like, and he was wailing and screaming and foaming at the mouth.

It reminded me of the first guy that Steve chased into the forest a few weeks ago.

It also kinda reminded me of my uncle Wither when he doesn't take his meds.

But, I accidently stepped on a branch, and he heard me.

Then he ran away really fast into the forest.

Man that was weird.

But villagers are weird most of the time, so guess I'm not surprised.

But I still don't know where Steve is.

And I need to find him too...

...I could sure use a friend right now.

Saturday

As I was walking out of the house today, my Mom asked me, "So where are you going?"

"Oh…Err… I'm just going to my friend's Ed's house. He lives around the school."

"Ed, huh? Do I know him? I know most of your friends. I've never heard of Ed."

"Oh, he's a new friend. I just met him. He's big and green and…Err…he's a really nice Zombie."

"Oh Ok. Well, have fun. Don't stay out too early or you'll get burned. Remember, the sun is coming up in a few hours."

"Thanks, Mom."

I still felt kind of weird lying to my Mom.

But I really needed to make some money to get my Harry Potter costume.

Plus, I really am going to visit my friend Ed. And he is big and green. He just happens to be Old Man Jenkin's horse, Ed, that's all.

Same thing. Right?

I walked over to the school where I found Old Man Jenkins mowing the lawn on the school soccer field.

"Hey there, Zombie, glad you could make it."

Old Man Jenkins was back in one piece again. But his whole chest and stomach were covered in Duct Tape.

"How are you doing, Mr. Jenkins?"

"Better than ever. Just needed a little Duct Tape and I'm as good as new."

"Oh Ok."

"Are you ready to take care of Ed?"

"I'm ready," I said.

Old Man Jenkins showed me everything that I needed to do to take care of his Zombie horse, Ed. It was a lot of hard work. The hardest part was taking off Ed's skin, dusting it, and then putting it back on.

But it was cool.

I wonder if regular Zombies can do that.

When I finally finished, Mr. Jenkins paid me a whole 30 bucks!

Wow, this is awesome. Now I just need to win the Scariest Costume Contest and

I'll have enough to buy my Harry Potter costume!

Mr. Jenkins said that Ed was not very friendly with strangers. He wouldn't let anyone ride him except Mr. Jenkins.

But I kind of liked Ed. He was really nice.

You know, I thought, *I bet you I could ride Ed too.*

So, when Mr. Jenkins wasn't around I thought I would see if I could sneak a ride.

I walked up real slow next to Ed, like I was going to pet him. Then I put my hand on his back and he stayed real still. Then I put both hands on his back, and he didn't move.

Then I jumped on Ed, and he just stood there.

Wow, he does like me!

Then I walked Ed around the soccer field a little bit.

Weeeeee! This is fun.

I wanted Ed to go a little faster so I kicked him really softly.

But after I did, something told me that Ed didn't like to be kicked.

All of a sudden Ed jumped up, kicked his back legs into the wall behind us, and took off.

I think he accidentally turned on the sprinkler system because all of a sudden there was water spraying all over the soccer field.

Then I realized that there was something that Ed hated more than getting kicked… And that was getting wet.

All of a sudden, Ed took off as fast as he could. And the wetter he got the faster he ran.

When the sprinklers finally stopped, Ed was soaking wet. And he had a really sad look on his face.

Oh man, oh man, oh man, oh man! I need to get Ed dry before Mr. Jenkins comes back. But what am I going to do?

I could tell that the sun was about to rise too, so I had to do something quick.

I got an idea!

I took off Ed's skin and I put it out on the grass.

Maybe the sun can dry it off, I thought.

The sun was just about to rise, so I led Ed into his cave and waited for the sun to dry his Zombie skin.

Next thing I know his Zombie horse skin burst into flames.

Oh no!

I was thinking of running out to get it, but it was too late. All that was left was a big piece of rotten Zombie flesh sizzling in the sun.

"What in tarnation happened to my horse?!!"

All of sudden, Old Man Jenkins showed up.

Everything inside me told me I should just tell Mr. Jenkins the truth.

But if I tell him the truth, I'm going to have to give back my $30. Then I'd never be able to get my Harry Potter Costume.

"Well, boy? What happened?"

"Uh, Mr. Jenkins, sir...Err... I led Ed back to the cave when the sun came up. But I think Ed saw a rabbit or something because he ran out into the grass, and then the sun made him catch on fire....."

"What? That's not like Ed. Then what happened?"

"Well, I lured him back into the cave. Then I took his skin off before it could burn him, and I threw it out onto the grass."

Mr. Jenkins looked at me with his big beady eye sockets. But I couldn't look at him, so I just looked at Ed, who had a really sad look on his face.

"Well, thank you so much!" Old Man Jenkins yelled as he patted me on the back. "I'm so glad you were here to save my best friend in the whole wide Overworld. If you weren't here, I don't know what I would've done."

Then he took out his wallet and pulled out 10 dollars.

"You deserve a reward for trying to save Ed. Here you go," Mr. Jenkins said.

Mr. Jenkins handed me the 10 dollars, and I just looked at it.

"Thanks again, Zombie, for being so brave."

"Uh...sure thing, Mr. Jenkins."

Then Mr. Jenkins and Ed walked away. And Ed turned around and gave me a really sad look.

I took the 10 dollars and I put it in my pocket.

And I just felt...terrible.

Sunday

I went to go see Steve to talk to him about what happened with Mr. Jenkins.

Something was telling me that I needed to go back and tell Mr. Jenkins the truth.

Come to think of it, I felt like I needed to go back and tell my parents the truth too.

But when I got to our usual hangout spot, Steve still wasn't there.

I checked all of the other places we hang out, but he wasn't there either.

I went by to see Alex again, except this time she wasn't there either.

Where is everybody? Was there a MineCon convention that I didn't know about or something?

I checked everywhere else I thought they could be and…nothing.

Man, what's going on?

Monday

"Zombie, we may be on time to your birthday party after all," my Mom said.

"Huh?"

"Well, there's a chance that Wesley's preschool trick-or-treating trip will start an hour late. So, that means your Dad and I can be here when your friends start showing up for your birthday party."

Oh man, this is terrible. I can't have my parents at my party when the cool kids from school show up!

"Uh, are you sure, Mom?"

"Well, I have to call Denise, Skelee's Mom, tonight to confirm it."

My Mom was busy feeding Wesley so I thought I would volunteer and find out if all my plans were going to be totally ruined.

"Mom, I can call Skelee's house for you if you want."

"Sure, that would be great, dear."

I called over to Skelee's house and Skelee answered.

"Wassup, bro?"

"Hey Zombie, what's up?"

"Hey, can you ask your mom if your little sister's preschool trick-or-treating trip is going to be an hour late?"

"Sure. Hold on… Hey, Mom! Is Tibia's trick-or-treating trip going to start an hour late? Zombie's Mom wants to know."

"Yes, it is!"

"Yeah, Zombie, they're going to start an hour late. Hey, does that mean that your parents are going to be there when your party starts?"

"Uh, don't remind me," I said. Then I hung up.

"Well, what did Denise say? Is the trick-or-treating trip going to start late?" my Mom asked.

Everything inside me told me I should just tell my Mom the truth.

But if my parents are here when all of the cool kids from school show up, they're all going to laugh at me and call me a "baby Zombie noob" or something.

"Uh… No, she said it's still going to be on time," I said.

"Really? I was sure it was going to start an hour late. Oh Ok. So I guess we're going to miss the start of your party. But you can

take care of things until we get back, right,
Zombie? Especially since you're a big Zombie
now. "

"Sure, no problem, Mom."

Well, I got what I wanted... .

...But, then why do I feel so bad about it?

Tuesday

Today, me and the guys went over to Ms. Ursula's house to grab the clown and take it to my house for my birthday party.

Since she wasn't around, I figured she wouldn't miss it.

When we got to Ms. Ursula's house, all her lights were off.

I was thinking of knocking on her door to see if she was there. But I was too scared to walk past the terrifying monster clown that was hovering in front of her doorway.

"Hey Skelee, why don't you go knock and see if she's there?"

99

"No way. I heard that clowns love eating bones for breakfast. "

"How about you, Slimey? You don't have any bones."

"No way. I heard clowns love JELLO. And if you didn't notice, I would make a really sweet midnight snack."

I was thinking of asking Creepy, but we all agreed that it probably wasn't a good idea.

"Why don't you throw a few rocks at her window to see if she's there?" Creepy suggested.

"Good idea."

So I picked up a few cobblestone rocks from her driveway.

Tick!

After I threw the first rock nothing happened.

"Maybe she's hard of hearing," Skelee said. "Throw a bigger one."

So I threw a bigger rock at her window.

Tack!

"She might be asleep, you know. You might need to wake her up," Slimey said.

So I picked up the biggest rock I could find.

KRESSSHHH!!

Ms. Ursula's window broke into like a million pieces.

"Oh man!"

We all ran behind the bushes to hide.

We waited to hear Ms. Ursula come running out of her house. But nothing happened.

"Hey, I don't think she's there," I said. "This is our chance to get the clown. Slimey, did you bring the sack?"

"Yeah, I got it right here. I couldn't find a sack so I just brought a pair of my Dad's work pants."

Slimey's Dad must be a big guy because those pants were huge.

So we slowly walked up to the clown.

But its beady little eyes were watching us every step of the way.

I had to close my eyes as I walked up to it. It was just too terrifying to watch. I noticed that the other guys had their eyes closed too.

We finally made it to the clown when suddenly we heard, "HE, HE, HE, HE, HE..."

"RUN! THE CLOWN'S ALIVE!!!"

The guys and I tried to run away but we all got caught in Slimey's Dad's workpants sack. We were all stuck in the sack and couldn't get out.

All we could hear was, "HE, HE, HE, HE, HE!"

"AAAAAAAHHH!!!! WE'RE GONNA DIE!!! THE CLOWN'S GOING TO EAT US!!!"

Then all of a sudden I felt a hand grab me by the collar and yank me out of the sack.

"IT'S GOT ME! I'M A GONNER!"

"What in tarnation are you boys doing?"

When I stopped screaming, I opened my eyes and I saw that it was Old Man Jenkins.

"Mr. Jenkins, save yourself! The clown's going to eat us all!!!"

Old Man Jenkins put his hand to his forehead and just shook his head like he usually does. Then he pulled out Skelee, Slimey and Creepy from the sack.

"What are you boy's talking about? This clown's not real. It's just 'electronical,' that's all."

"Really?"

"Yeah, watch." Then Mr. Jenkins waved his hand in front of the clown and it said, "HE, HE, HE, HE, HE…"

Me and the guys jumped behind Mr. Jenkins when the clown spoke.

Then we all looked at each other.

"PFFFFFTTTTT!!!!" was all we could say and then we burst out laughing.

Creepy was hissing and flashing, but when we started laughing he calmed down.

"What were you boys doing here anyway?"
Mr. Jenkins asked.

Everything inside me told me I should just tell
Mr. Jenkins the truth.

*But if he tells my Mom and Dad what we
were up to, I'll be grounded for like a month.
And then they won't let me have my birthday
party.*

"Uh… We were just walking by and we heard
a scream," I said. "We thought Ms. Ursula
was being attacked by the clown monster. So
we brought a sack to capture it and save Ms.
Ursula."

All the guys looked at me with a surprised
look.

Mr. Jenkins lifted up what remained of one
of his eyebrows. He looked around at the
clown, the sack, the window and then at us.

Then he said, "Well done, boy! It's a good thing we have such heroic boys like you to protect everyone in this town."

Me and the guys all looked at each other... surprised.

"And I think that kind of bravery deserves a reward."

Mr. Jenkins dug into his saddle bag that was on Ed, his horse. Then he pulled out some Halloween candy he had just bought.

"Here you go," he said as he handed us each some candy.

"Thanks, Mr. Jenkins," we all said.

"No, thank you boys, for being so brave," he said.

Then Mr. Jenkins walked away with Ed, his horse.

And Ed turned and looked at us with a really sad look on his face.

Then me and the guys all looked at each other.

We unwrapped the candy and put it in our mouths.

And we all felt...terrible.

Wednesday

"**D**id you see Jeff's costume? It's like sooooooo scary!"

That's all I heard from a bunch of the kids at school today.

"What's your costume going to be, Zombie?"

I know I should've just said that I haven't got my costume yet.

But then they're going to think that I'm just a big fake, baby, phony, noob, I thought.

"Oh man! My costume is the scariest, most hideous costume you've ever seen. I'm totally going to win the Scariest Costume Contest," I said.

"Really? What is it?"

"Uh… It's so scary that…err… There aren't any words to describe what is!" I said.

Some of the kids just gave me a strange look and walked away.

Man, the Scariest Costume Contest is in just a few days.

And I need to come up with a costume quick!

And it's got to be an awesome costume too. It's the only way I can beat Jeff and win that $50 Zombies R Us gift certificate.

But what am I going to do?

C'mon think, Zombie, think!

Thursday

I got it!

I was scrolling through my Mom's camera and I remembered that I had the perfect costume all along.

Since Wesley is not going to need his costume till Saturday, I think I'm going to borrow it for the Scariest Costume Contest tomorrow.

I just have to figure out how to make it fit.

Hmmm... A pair of scissors, some Duct Tape and some of Mom's black tights should do the trick.

After cutting and stretching, and taping, I finally finished.

Now I just need to put it on and see what it looks like in the mirror...

Just like I thought, awesome!

Man, I'm gonna win that Scariest Costume Contest for sure!

Friday

Most of the kids came to school in their costumes today.

It was weird. It looked like a scene from a scary movie I saw with Steve once.

I think it he said it was called "The Wizard of Oz."

We had the big Halloween Party in the school gym.

It was so cool.

They had cookies and milk, and all sorts of games. They even redecorated the whole gym to look like a human village.

Oooooh…so creepy.

A lot of the kids were dressed like villagers.

They looked so real I felt like sneaking up to them and scaring them.

One kid even started talking like them...

"Hurrr... Hurrr..." was all he said as he walked around.

They even had a huge life-sized statue of an
Iron Golem.

Man that thing brought back scary
memories...

I didn't wear my costume because I wanted to wait till the Scariest Costume Contest started to bring it out.

So I went to get some milk and cookies and wait for the guys to show up.

All of a sudden the scariest monster that I had ever seen jumped out from behind the curtains.

"RRAAAAARRRRGGHHHH!"

115

"AAAAAHHHH!!!!!"

All the milk I drank went right through me.

All of the other kids started laughing.

"Ha, ha! I guess you're not so brave after all!" Big Mouth Jeff said.

"Wha… Is that you, Jeff?!!!"

"I told you I had the scariest costume ever. That $50 gift certificate is going to be all mine."

Then he walked away and started scaring other kids.

Man, Jeff's costume was really scary. He might just win the contest. What am I going to do?

Wow, I feel really bummed right now.

Man, where's Steve? I know that if he were here, he would know what to say to cheer me up.

Hmmm…. Maybe I can make believe like he is here…

I bet if I use my Steve voice I could think about what he would say…

"Hey Zombie, what's eating you?" I said in my best Steve voice.

"Nothing, just maggots."

"No, I mean what's wrong?"

"I think I'm going to lose the Scariest Costume Contest and then I won't be able to buy my Harry Potter costume."

"And if you don't get your Harry Potter costume, what's gonna happen?"

"Then the cool kids at school will think my party is lame."

"What will your real friends think, Zombie?"

"Oh those guys don't care about that stuff. They just want to spend time with me and have fun with me at my party."

"Which is more fun? Looking good for the cool kids or spending time with your best pals?"

"Whoa! Steve, you're so deep."

"Yeah, I know... It's because I have a big square head and I punch trees..."

Wow, I feel a whole lot better. Who would 'a thought that Steve could help me even though he's not around?

"ALL THE KIDS WHO ARE GOING TO ENTER THE SCARIEST COSTUME CONTEST,

PLEASE MAKE YOUR WAY TO THE STAGE," the announcement said.

Well, here's my chance.

So I went behind the back curtain to put on my costume. They started calling out names so that the kids could show off their costumes to the audience. I stayed behind the curtain until they called my name.

"Linus Enderbottom."

"RAAARRR!"

"Yeah!" the crowd cheered.

"Lucy Zombironi."

"Hello!"

"Yeah!" the crowd cheered.

"Wilbur Ghast Tentacles."

"Walalalah!"

"Whoa!" the crowd cheered.

"Manny Festation."

"Boo!"

"Yeah!"

So far, it doesn't sound like any of costumes are really scary. I guess that means it's going be a battle between me and Jeff.

"Rick Amortis."

"Uuuurrgghhh!"

"Boooo! Lame! So unoriginal!"

"Zack Zombie."

Well, here goes nothing...

"Wah, wah, wah, wah, wah!" I yelled in my best human baby voice.

"Gasp! Huh! Oh! Gulp!"

The audience got quiet. All of the kids and teachers just stared with their eye sockets wide open.

Then all of a sudden...

"YEEAAHHHHHH!!!!!!!"

All the kids and teachers started clapping and cheering for my costume.

Oh man, I think I'm gonna win!

"And our last contestant is Rupert Jeffery Carcass the Third..."

"RRRAAAAAARRRRRGGGGHHHH!!!"

"AAAAAHHHHH!!!!! Run for your lives! It's the Zombie Apocalypse!"

All the kids and teachers started running and screaming all over the place. Some of the kids knocked over the tables, and food was flying through the air.

"Attention, Attention students! It's OK, it is only a costume!" the principal said.

Then all of the kids and teachers came out of their hiding places.

"Well, Jeffrey, I guess it is obvious that you have the scariest costume in the whole school. So I'm happy to announce that you are the winner of our annual Halloween Scariest Costume Contest."

"Yeah!" All of the kids cheered for Jeffrey as he got his trophy and his $50 Zombies R Us gift certificate.

122

I was a little sad that I didn't win the contest and get the gift certificate.

But you know, I really didn't feel that bad about it.

"Hey Zombie, cool costume," Skelee said. "Are you going to wear that at your party tomorrow?"

"I guess I am," I said.

"That's great. I was thinking of wearing a costume tomorrow that might be scarier than yours. Check it out." Skelee showed me a picture of his costume.

"Whoa! That's terrifying."

"Yeah, Slimey and Creepy have some really scary costumes too," Skelee said. "We can't wait for your party tomorrow."

"Yeah, it's going to be the scariest party ever."

Me and the guys all laughed. Then we filled up on more cookies and milk.

Saturday—
My Birthday!

Happy Birthday, Me!

That's right. Today's my birthday. October 31ˢᵗ, Halloween.

And now I'm 13 years old.

It's funny because I don't feel any older.

I thought I would check myself out in the mirror to see if I grew a mold mustache overnight or something.

But when I looked in the mirror I was kind of bummed.

No mustache.

I did see a little more mold on my chin, though.

And, I lost a few more of my eyebrows.

But I was kind of expecting something really cool like a few more holes in my face or something.

Nothing...just more dimples.

I did notice that my left leg grew a few inches last night.

So now both my legs are almost the same size.

Of course that means that I'm walking straight again like a human.

Uuurrrgghhh! I wish my body knew what it was doing.

Man, puberty is so hard for a young Zombie.

But I don't care about all that, because today I'm having my birthday party.

I decided to give up the Harry Potter theme idea.

Me and the guys decided to do a "Scariest Party Ever" instead.

My mom is even going to make some really cool food that looks like scary stuff.

She's going to make worms that look like human fingers.

…And slime cupcakes that look like boogers.

…And cookies that look like spider eyes.

And she's even going to make a cake that looks like brains!

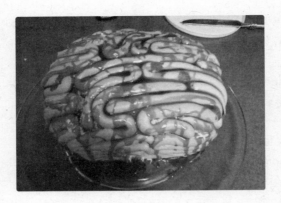

Yeah, gross I know. It's going to be awesome!

When I got downstairs my Mom, Dad and Wesley were eating breakfast.

"Happy Birthday, Zombie!" my Mom and Dad said.

"Habby Burtday Zumbie!" Wesley said.

"How does it feel to be a whole 13 years old, Zombie?"

"It feels OK, I guess."

"I see you lost more of your eyebrows last night. Any other big Zombie changes happen?"

"Not really, Dad."

I wanted to tell him about my extra chin mold, but my Dad would've probably made a big deal about it.

"I remember when I turned 13," my Dad said. "I really wanted to grow a mold mustache but I couldn't. So I just let my nose hairs grow really long and it looked just as good. Eating was a bit of a problem, but I eventually got used to it."

Man. My parents are so weird.

But, I got my whole schedule all set up for today.

First my Mom is going to take me to Zombies R Us to buy some more stuff for my birthday

Party. And she needed to get another costume for Wesley since I kind of destroyed his.

She wasn't too happy I took Wesley's costume. But I think she forgot about it once she saw that Wesley and I were going to have matching costumes this Halloween.

"Oh, you're both so cute," she said.

Parents are so weird.

After that, I'm coming home and setting up all of the decorations for my party.

Then I promised my Mom and Dad I would help get Wesley ready for his trick-or-treating trip. I kind of felt bad because I didn't tell my Mom and Dad that Wesley's trick or treating trip was going to start late.

But I really didn't want my parents here when the cool kids showed up to my party.

Anyway, after that, I'm going to change into my costume and wait for all of the kids from school to come to my Halloween party.

Wow, this is going to be the best night of my life.

Things couldn't get any better.

Saturday
Midday Entry

The weirdest thing happened on our way back from Zombies R Us.

I saw a bunch of mob kids running around with Pumpkin Head costumes like Big Mouth Jeff had.

Wow, that must be a really popular costume this year, I thought.

When we got home Mom started making all of the cool food for my Halloween party, while Dad and I started putting up decorations.

"I see you got the new blow up Snow Golem doll for the front yard," My Dad said.

"Yeah, and when you pass by it, it moves its arms up and down like it's going to crush you."

"You know, when I was a boy we had a blow up human mailman doll that we put up in our front yard on Halloween. Whenever you passed by, it would hand you your mail. And let me tell you, that was pretty scary."

Wow, my parents are so weird.

When we finished putting up the decorations, my house looked awesome!

It was so scary that I got really nervous when my parents were about to leave to take Wesley trick-or-treating.

"Are you sure you're going to be OK all by yourself, Zombie? One of us could stay behind until your friends get here."

"No, that's OK, Mom. I'm a big Zombie now. I can take care of things until the guys get here," I said nervously.

"All right. We'll see you in a few hours."

So there I was, all by myself in my spooky house on Halloween.

I guess I'm just being paranoid, I thought.

I mean really, what could go wrong?

Saturday Night Entry

"**K**nock, Knock, Knock!"

Oh cool, the guys are here. Let's get this party started!

"Trick or treat!"

"AAAAAHHHHHH!!!"

"Happy Birthday Zombie!" Skelee, Slimey and Creepy said.

"Wow, your costumes are so scary!"

The guys weren't kidding when they said they were going to have scary costumes.

Skelee dressed up in his flower baby costume.

Slimey dressed up like a butterfly.

And Creepy dressed up like a pea in a pod.

So scary.

"Is anybody else coming to your party?"
Creepy asked.

"Yeah, a ton of the kids from school are supposed to come. It's going to be the best party ever."

"Whoa!" the guys said.

"Hey, where are the milk and cookies?" Slimey asked.

Me and the guys jumped in and started eating some of the cool snacks my Mom made.

"Yeah, we even have a cake that looks like brains."

"Gross!" the guys said.

After we ate, we started watching some T.V.

Man, where is everybody? It's already been like an hour and nobody else has shown up yet.

"I thought you said more kids were coming to your party?" Skelee asked.

"Yeah. They'll be here any minute. They're just…Err…running late… He, he."

All of a sudden we heard a loud knock at the door.

THUMP!...THUMP!...THUMP!...

"See they're here!"

I was so glad somebody finally made it. For a minute there I thought nobody was coming

But when I opened the door, I couldn't believe who it was.

"RAAAAGGGHHRRR!"

"Jeff, what are you doing here? I never invited… I mean… I never thought you were coming to my party."

Even though I didn't like Big Mouth Jeff much, I was just glad somebody came to my party.

And he was wearing his pumpkin head costume so it kind of fit in with our "Scariest Party Ever" theme.

"RAAAAGGGHHRRR!"

"Whoa! That's really scary Jeff. Great costume," Skelee said.

"RAAAAGGGHHRRR!"

"So realistic!" Slimey said.

"RAAAAGGGHHRRR!"

"And it's really scary how you keep saying, RAAGGHHRR and stuff," Creepy said.

"RAAAAGGGHHRRR!"

"Hey, you want some food?" I asked Jeff. "We got human worm fingers, booger cupcakes, spider eye cookies…"

"RAAAAGGGHHRRR!"

"And we have a cake that looks like…brains!"

"RAUUH?"

"Yeah, gross right? My Mom made it. Dig in."

Jeff started sniffing around the brain cake real weird like. But Jeff was always weird, so I guess it was OK.

"BRRAINNSS?"

"Yeah, it looks just like brains. Cool right?"

"BBRRRAAAIIIINNNNSSSS!!!!!"

All of a sudden, pumpkin head Jeff started screaming and wailing and chomping on the cake.

"Whoa. Calm down there, killer. We need to save some for the rest of the guests."

"RAAAAGGGHHRRR!!!!
BBBRRAAIINNSSS!!!"

"Uh, Zombie... Something tells me that's not Jeff," Skelee said as he pointed to the T.V. set.

I looked at the T.V. and they were showing some kind of emergency broadcast.

EMERGENCY ALERT SYSTEM

ALERT

PLEASE STAND BY

"I repeat… You can identify the infected by the large pumpkin that has spawned on their head. If you encounter one of the infected we warn you to stay as far away from them as you can. The infection is highly contagious and is spread through a bite. So protective clothing is suggested…"

"RAAAAGGGHHRRR!!!! BBBRRAAIINNSSS!!!"

"AAAAAAHHHHH!!!!!" we yelled.

As the Pumpkin Head monster thing ate the brain cake, me and the guys locked ourselves in the bathroom.

"What are we going to do?" Creepy said hissing.

"I don't know," I said.

All we could hear on the other side of the bathroom door was, "RAAAAGGGHHRRR!!!! BBBRRAAIINNSSS!!!"

"Hey, you still have Slimey's Dad's workpants sack from the other night?" Skelee asked me.

"Yeah, it's in the closet."

"Why don't we use that to grab Pumpkin Head and lock him in the closet?"

"Great idea. But we better do it fast before the brain cake runs out."

"I'm really scared, Zombie," Creepy said.

"Me too, Creepy... But let's do this!"

We all jumped out of the bathroom and ran to the closet.

Pumpkin Head was still devouring the cake, so we snuck really quietly and got the sack out of the closet.

Then we all grabbed a corner of the sack and walked slowly behind him.

"Alright guys," I whispered, "On the count of three... One... Two... Three... NOW!!!"

"RAAAAGGHRR!!!... UUMMPPHH!..."

We got Pumpkin Head in the sack and then we pushed him in the closet and locked it.

"RRAAGGHHRRR!!! THUMP! THUMP! THUMP!"

But Pumpkin Head was still trying to get out.

144

"Quick, help me move the couch in front of the closet," I said.

After we put the couch in front of the closet, me and the guys just sat down on the couch exhausted.

"Whoa. That was intense!" Skelee said.

"Uh...guys...I don't think it's over..." Slimey said pointing to the T.V.

We all looked at the T.V. and saw pictures of pumpkin headed mobs chasing folks all around the neighborhood.

"Hey, turn it up!"

"*...not able to contain the infected. We repeat... The Zombie police are not able to contain the infected. We therefore encourage residents to find safety at the Mob Village Middle School. I repeat, if you have not been* bitten you can find safety at the Mob Village Middle School...

...This is serious folks. Sources say that this epidemic may be the beginning of the next Zombie Apocalypse...

...Huh? What's that noise? How'd they get in here? RUN!!!"

"RRAAAAAGGHHRRR!!!"

"...BEEEEEEEEEEPPP..."

Then all that was left on the T.V. was static.

"Oh man. What are we going to do?" Creepy asked.

"You heard the news. We need to make it to the Middle School. We'll be safe there," I said.

"Yeah...but for how long?" Skelee asked.

Then all of us just looked at each other... worried.

So we planned to make a run for the school. We grabbed anything we could find to defend ourselves against the Pumpkin Heads. But we weren't sure if we were even going to make it.

But the thing that was really bothering me was that my Mom, Dad and Wesley were out there.

Man, if I had told Mom and Dad the truth, they would still be safe with us right here, I thought.

Because I lied, my Mom, Dad and Wesley could be really hurt right now.

Man, what am I going to do?

"Zombie, are you ready?" Skelee asked.

I looked at all the guys who were covered in pots and pans from head to toe.

I thought about my Mom, Dad and Wesley. If they were still OK, I had to go save them.

I thought about my best pals that really needed me right now.

And I thought about Steve, who I knew somehow, somewhere, needed my help.

And I knew that if there was ever a time to quit, if there was ever a time to give up, if there was ever a time to throw in the towel, this was not it!

"Let's do this!"

Saturday
Late Night Entry

We barely made it to the school.

All we saw on the way were Pumpkin Heads chasing screaming mob folks up and down the neighborhood.

But when we finally made it to the school... there was nobody there.

"Where is everybody?" I asked.

"I don't know… They said to come to our Middle School, right?" Slimey asked.

"Yeah, but I don't think anybody else made it," Skelee said.

All of a sudden we heard noises coming.

"RRRAAAAAGGGHHHRRRR!!!"

"Did you hear that? Quick, let's hide!" I said.

We ran down the school hallway, checking all of the classroom doors to see which ones were open.

Creepy and I found one at the end of the hall, and Skelee and Slimey jumped into another open classroom close by.

"Quick, Creepy, hide in the closet," I said.

I was trying my best to keep Creepy calm. But he was hissing so much. Even his liquid Nitrogen inhaler wasn't helping.

"RRRAAAAAGGGHHHRRRR!!!"

The Pumpkin Heads were right at the door. I locked Creepy in the closet, and then I jumped behind the teacher's desk hoping they wouldn't find me.

The door slowly opened, and I heard two of them come in.

"RRRAAAAAGGGHHHRRRR!!!" was all they said as they slowly walked around the classroom.

I could feel the maggots stand up on the back of my neck as they got closer and closer.

Oh man. This is it. I thought. *I'm not going to make it.*

All I could think about was my Mom, Dad and Wesley.

I'm not going to be able to save them, I thought. *And I'll never be able to tell them how sorry I am for lying to them...*

Then the Pumpkin Heads found me.

"RRRAAAAAGGGHHHRRRR!!!"

Goodbye cruel world...

"You're not going to give up that easily are you?"

"Wha...?"

"I thought I taught you better than that."

"Huh?"

Then the monster standing over me took off its big pumpkin head and it was...

152

"STEVE!!!!"

"That's right. In the flesh."

Then the other monster took off its pumpkin head and it was…

"ALEX!!!"

"That's me."

"But what…? When…? Where…? How?!!!"

"I know you got a lot of questions, Zombie, but we need to get out of here fast. Who else did you bring?"

"Just Creepy. I locked him in the closet. And Skelee and Slimey are in the classroom across the hall.

"All right, let's get those guys and head over to the Potions Brewing Lab, now!"

Sunday
Early Entry

We got to the Potions Brewing Lab, but by then the sun already started coming up.

"Quick, Alex, pull down the blinds," Steve said.

Steve and Alex pulled the blinds down so that the sunlight wouldn't hurt me and Skelee.

When we walked in the classroom somebody was already in there brewing something in a cauldron.

"Hello, Zombie."

"Ms. Ursula!!!"

It was Ms. Ursula, my neighbor the witch, brewing something.

"I'm glad you were able to make it safely to the school. You're a pretty tough Zombie... even against clowns."

"Uh...yeah. Sorry about that, Ms. Ursula.

"Ms. Ursula is brewing a counter spell to cure the Pumpkin Heads," Steve said.

"Is it working?"

"Yes, but I am going to need more time," Ms. Ursula said. "Also, I need the full moon in order to give the potion its power. And the next full moon comes out tonight."

I had so many questions for Steve I didn't even know where to begin.

"So Steve, what's going on?"

"Well, for starters, everything that's happening in your Mob village already happened in our village. Alex and I are the only humans in our village that didn't get infected."

"But, how did you get away?"

"Well, it was all thanks to Alex actually."

"Yep. All me," Alex said.

"You see, when I went to go find the missing villagers I eventually found them. But they weren't too happy to see me. Actually, those Pumpkin Heads chased me all the way into a cave. Then one of the Pumpkin Heads found me and I thought I was a goner. But, next thing I know, Alex is standing over me laughing, with a pumpkin on her head."

"Yeah, I really had him going for a while there," Alex said.

"It seems that the infected can't tell who you are if you put a pumpkin on your head," Steve said.

"Kinda like an Endermen?"

"Yep. So we've just been wearing pumpkin heads and walking around, hoping we could find survivors."

"But we didn't find any survivors in our village," Alex said. "Our whole village is totally infected."

"So me and Alex tried to get help to find a cure for the Pumpkin Heads. I remembered how Belinda the Jungle Witch helped us before. But the problem was that she wasn't around. So, I came to find the only other witch that I knew about, your neighbor, Ms. Ursula."

"After Steve and Alex came to see me, I had to travel to the different biomes to get all of the ingredients that I needed," Ms. Ursula said.

"So that's why they said you were missing!" I exclaimed. "And that's why you weren't there when I broke your window."

"What window?"

"Oh...err...nothing."

Wow, that was a crazy story. But I was just so happy to see Steve again. Life just wasn't the same without him.

"Hey Zombie, you ready to see your parents? They've been really worried about you," Steve said.

"My parents?!!! They're here?!!!"

"Yeah, a lot of the parents are in the gymnasium. I'm sure they're going to be really happy to see all of you guys."

Then Steve, the guys and I ran downstairs to the gymnasium in the basement.

When we opened the doors, there were a bunch of mobs from the neighborhood there.

We found Skelee's parents, Slimey's parents, and Creepy's family was all there too.

I saw my Mom and Dad from far away and I ran to them.

"Mom! Dad!"

"Zombie! You're safe! We were so worried about you!"

I gave my parents the biggest hug ever.

"Habby Burtday Zumbie!"

"Wesley!"

I gave Wesley the biggest hug ever, too.

"Mom…Dad… I am so sorry for lying to you about Wesley's trick-or-treating trip. I never meant for you to get hurt. I just wanted to look good in front of my friends. Now I know how dumb that was. And I promise I will never, ever lie to you again!"

"Zombie, we already forgave you when we found out that you lied to us," Mom said.

"What? How did you know?"

"Well, Denise called me later this week to make arrangements for the trip. She told me about the time change," Mom said.

"Yes, son. We've known something was wrong ever since Mr. Jenkins told us that you were sneaking over to work with him on the weekends," my Dad said. "He also told us about the lie you told him about burning the skin off of his Zombie horse. And, he even told us that you lied about Ms. Ursula's clown, and her broken window."

"Really? You knew about all that? But, how come you didn't say anything?"

"Well, Zombie. We talked it over with Mr. Jenkins and we figured that you needed to sort out those situations for yourself," my Mom said. "And we believed in you."

"Yes, son," my Dad said. "We knew that you would eventually choose the right course. And eventually, you did."

Wow... My parents are so cool.

Man, even in the middle of a Zombie Apocalypse, I just realized that I am the luckiest Zombie in the whole world.

Oh no! Mr. Jenkins!!!

"Mom, Dad... Did Mr. Jenkins make it?"

"Sort of..." Dad said. "He's over there."

When I looked over I saw Old Man Jenkins napping next to Ed, his Zombie horse...

...Well, his top half anyway. I guess the Duct Tape wasn't strong enough to survive a Zombie Apocalypse.

I was just so happy that everyone was OK that I jumped on my parents one more time and gave them a really big hug.

Then, because I was so tired, I just fell asleep.

Sunday
Midday Entry

"Wake up, Zombie, it's almost sundown," Steve said.

When I woke up, I was hoping that everything that had happened was just a really bad dream.

But, it wasn't.

I was still in the school gymnasium with all of the other parents and kids from the neighborhood.

"Are the Pumpkin Heads still out there?" I asked Steve.

"Yep. And now there are more than ever."

"But shouldn't the sun have burned them to a crisp by now?"

"I thought so too. But it looks like the pumpkins protect them from getting burned somehow," Steve said.

We all ran up to the Potions Brewing Lab to see if Ms. Ursula was finished with the cure.

"As soon as the sun goes down, and the full moon comes out, the potion will be ready," Ms. Ursula said.

"But is that going to be enough to help the whole town?" I asked. "And what about Steve's village?"

"You'll have to dilute it in water and then sprinkle it on all of the infected," she said.

"How are we going to do that?" Alex asked.

We were all thinking of different ways that we could get the potion on the Pumpkin Heads. Best idea we came up with was to use a few super soakers that we found in the school's lost and found.

"I got it!" I said. "How about using the sprinkler system? We can put the potion in the school's water supply and then sprinkle the whole soccer field."

"That's great, Genius. But how are we supposed to get all of the Pumpkin Heads to all come to the soccer field?" Alex asked.

"Somebody is going to have to go throughout town, get their attention and lure them back here," Steve said.

I thought about Old Man Jenkins and his Zombie Horse, Ed. But since Mr. Jenkins was only half the Zombie he used to be, I realized that it was going to be up to me.

"I'll do it," I said. "I'll just ride Ed, the Zombie horse, throughout town and get the Pumpkin Heads to chase me back here."

"Way to go, Zombie!" Steve said. "That settles it. Alex, you and Ms. Ursula get the potion to the school's water supply that's connected to the sprinkler system. The guys and I will keep the rest of the Pumpkin Heads busy on the soccer field. Right, guys?"

"Gulp! Uh, yeah sure…" the guys said.

"Except you, Creepy, you can sit this one out," Steve said.

I told my Mom and Dad what I had to do. They didn't like it, but they knew it was the only way to help save everybody.

I stooped down and asked Old Man Jenkins if I could borrow Ed for one last ride.

"You're a really weird Zombie, you know that? But I reckon that you're ready." Then Mr. Jenkins put his hand on my shoulder and his eye sockets started tearing up. "I've always believed in you, Zombie... Just bring back Ed in one piece, OK?"

"You can count on it, Mr. Jenkins."

I jumped on Ed and rode out of the gymnasium and over to the main doors of the school.

"All right guys. This is it!" Steve said. "Everybody is counting on us. And not just mobs, but humans too. We can't fail, because there is too much at stake. So, if there was ever a time to quit, if there was ever a time to give up, if there was ever a time to throw in the towel, this is not it!"

I knew I heard that speech before.

"Are you guys ready?!!!"

"YEAH!!!"

"Let's do this!!!"

Sunday
Night Entry

I don't know what I was thinking.

But there I was, riding Ed, the Zombie horse, and kicking him as hard as I could to get him to go faster.

And behind us were a couple hundred screaming Pumpkin Heads chasing us as fast as they could.

And, it seemed like no matter how fast we went, the Pumpkin Heads were getting closer and closer.

But, I finally saw a glimpse of the Middle School from far away. And then I saw the soccer field.

There were already a few hundred more Pumpkin Heads on the soccer field running around. And it looked like they were chasing something.

When I got closer, I noticed that they were chasing Steve, Skelee and Slimey, who were running round and round, all over the field.

Then, I guess the guys must have seen me because next thing I know they took off into the school as fast as they could.

As soon as I reached the soccer field, the Pumpkin Heads forgot about Steve and the guys and turned their attention to me and Ed.

"Get ready, Alex!" Steve yelled.

Alex was perched next to the sprinkler system, ready to turn it on.

So right when I reached the edge of the soccer field, and the big crowd of unfriendly

170

Pumpkin Heads were waiting to jump on me and Ed, Steve yelled, "NOW!!!"

All of sudden the sprinkler system went off, and a burst of purplish liquid started spraying on every Pumpkin Head in the soccer field.

The sprinklers got Ed wet too, which made him run faster and faster.

It was a good thing too. He was running so fast that the big crowd of Pumpkin Heads couldn't catch us.

Man, I hope this works, I thought.

As the sprinkler system soaked the crowd, all of the Pumpkin Heads started wailing and screaming.

"RAAAGGGHHHRRR!!!! RRAAAAGGHHRR!!!! RRAAAAGGHHRR!!!!" was all they said.

Then little by little, the screams began to die down.

Next thing you know, the Pumpkin Heads began doing weird things with their arms and legs.

And then suddenly their Pumpkin Heads started shrinking!

First they went from having large pumpkin heads, to small pumpkin heads, to just small traces of pumpkin on their heads, until finally the pumpkins were gone.

It worked!

I rode Ed in through the main doors of the Middle School and down to the basement, where Steve, Alex, Ms. Ursula and the guys were waiting.

"Well, did it work?" Steve asked.

"It sure did. It looks like everybody is going back to normal," I said.

"YEAHHHH!!!!" All of the mobs and their families cheered as they celebrated and hugged each other.

"Whew! For a minute there I thought we would have to go back to living in caves," Skelee said.

"Well if we did, at least we would have had plenty of pumpkin pie to eat," Steve said.

Then all of us just burst out laughing.

Monday

After most of the town was cured on the soccer field, Ms. Ursula brewed some more of her potion to use on the remaining Mobs residents.

Ms. Ursula also made a special batch for Steve's village. Then, armed with a whole truckload of super soakers, Steve, Alex the guys and I, along with a bunch of the residents from Mob village, went over to Steve's village and helped cure all of the infected villagers.

The humans from Steve's village were so grateful that they made peace with all the mobs from Mob Village. They even made Halloween their national holiday, to remind them of the day that humans and mobs worked together to save the Overworld.

Now, Halloween became the one night of the year that humans and mobs could hang out together without scaring each other. So, on Halloween, humans and mobs put aside their differences, and they dress up like one another to show their appreciation. They even visit each other's homes and eat together.

So cool…

As for me, it was the best birthday that I've ever had.

It was also the craziest experience of my life, and I'm going to never forget it.

I'm also never going to forget that no matter how tough life gets, lying doesn't fix anything. Because even though lying is really, really easy, it sure makes life really, really hard.

Instead, I learned that trusting the people that love you and believe in you, is what will really help save the day.

So even though I just barely made it through a Zombie Apocalypse…

When I think about my Mom, my Dad, and my little brother Wesley…

And I think about my best buds Skelee, Slimey and Creepy…

And I think about my ghoulfriend Sally, and my crazy, tough as nails friend Alex…

And when I especially think about my best friend Steve…

I realize that no matter how crazy my young Zombie life gets…

With family and friends like these… I'm the luckiest Zombie in the whole wide Overworld.

The End